Antarctica
The Last Great Wilderness

Coral Tulloch

Rigby

Our earth is often called the Blue Planet. Seen from space, Earth is almost covered by blue oceans. The large masses of land in the blue seas are the continents.

In the south, a large white continent covered in ice reflects the sun's light. This is Antarctica.

Coral Tulloch went there. In this interview, she talks to us about her wonderful journey.

Mawson Station, Antarctica, is one of the oldest scientific research bases on the continent.

Coral, why did you want to go to Antarctica, and how were you able to go there?

I write and illustrate stories for children, and I wanted to write about Antarctica, the last great **wilderness**.

I was accepted as an **expeditioner** with ANARE, the Australian National Antarctic Research **Expeditions**.

On my voyage on the ice-breaker *Aurora Australis,* we visited four of Australia's five Antarctic bases.

The *Aurora Australis* approaches the Amery Ice Shelf.

Coral, why is Antarctica often called "the last great wilderness"?

Because Antarctica is isolated, wild, and unspoiled. Nobody really lives in Antarctica. The only people who visit there for long periods are scientists and the people who work with them.

Coral, what is Antarctica like?

Antarctica's mountains, buried under ice, rise to form the highest **plateau** in the world. Fierce winds that start here make their way back to the ocean and affect the climate of the whole planet. It is the coldest, windiest, highest, driest, cleanest, and loneliest place on Earth.

Why do you say it's the driest place on Earth? Doesn't it rain there?

No. It's too cold for rain! Only snow falls. In winter, it's dark for most of the day, and temperatures drop so low that even the ocean freezes. When the oceans freeze in winter, Antarctica is one and one-half times the size of North America.

In the middle of summer, the nights are as light as the days. The sea ice begins to melt, and ships are able to get closer to the land. This is when some of the scientists and other workers can go home, and new people come.

Even the animals in Antarctica come and go with the seasons.

Did you go to the South Pole?

Oh, no! That's a very difficult journey, over hundreds of miles of ice. Almost all of Antarctica is covered with ice. The ice is called the **polar** ice cap. In some places, the ice is nearly two miles thick and as hard as steel.

The five Australian bases are located at Heard Island, Macquarie Island, Casey, Davis, and Mawson.

below: Inside a giant crack in the ice

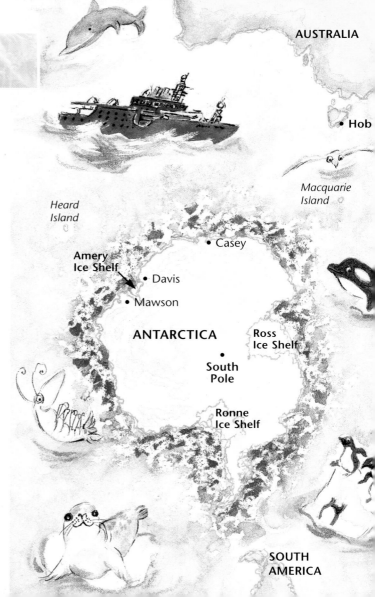

AUSTRALIA

• Hob

Macquarie Island

Heard Island

• Casey

Amery Ice Shelf

• Davis

• Mawson

ANTARCTICA

Ross Ice Shelf

South Pole

Ronne Ice Shelf

SOUTH AMERICA

How did the polar ice cap get so thick?

It has been growing for hundreds of thousands of years. As the snow falls, it piles on top of the existing snow, pressing the snow underneath into ice.

The ice flows slowly across the continent, moving all the time. At the edges, it forms **ice shelves** and **glaciers**.

This photograph, taken from space, shows the Darwin and the Byrd Glaciers, which flow onto the Ross Ice Shelf.

Ross Ice Shelf

Darwin Glacier

Byrd Glacier

What is a glacier? And where do icebergs come from?

A glacier is like a river of ice, moving very slowly across the land.

Under the pressure of the moving ice and the pounding summer sea, bits of glaciers and ice shelves break off and become icebergs. Some icebergs are as large as small cities and can take years to melt as they float in the ocean.

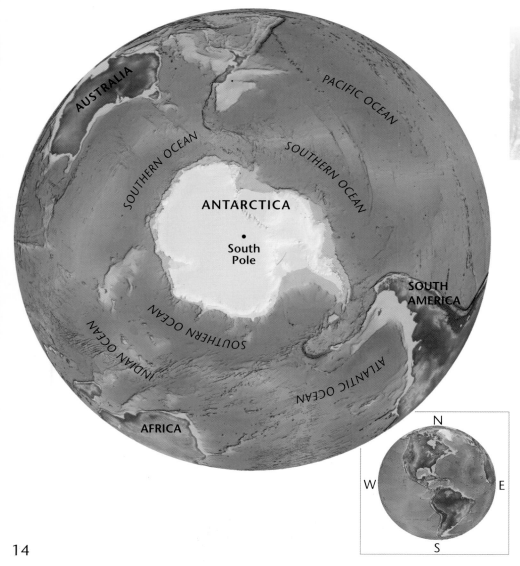

AUSTRALIA

PACIFIC OCEAN

SOUTHERN OCEAN

SOUTHERN OCEAN

ANTARCTICA

• South Pole

SOUTHERN OCEAN

INDIAN OCEAN

ATLANTIC OCEAN

SOUTH AMERICA

AFRICA

N

W E

S

Is it true that all the great oceans of the world meet around Antarctica?

Yes, this is where the Pacific, the Indian, and the Atlantic Ocean meet, in the Southern Ocean. When these warm, **moist** ocean waters and air meet the cold water and air of Antarctica, wild storms are created.

Freezing and melting and whipped by winds, the Southern Ocean swirls around Antarctica. It carries water, heat, and salt between the oceans of the world. Because it is so important, scientists are studying the ways that the Southern Ocean affects the whole planet.

A ship meets the waves of the Southern Ocean.

How do plants and animals survive in Antarctica?

Seals, penguins, and whales all have a thick layer of **blubber** under their skins to protect them from the cold.

Some Antarctic fish make a kind of **antifreeze** in their bodies that stops their blood from freezing.

All of these creatures depend on the ocean for their food. Nothing grows on the land except tiny plants, such as mosses, which grow very slowly and can survive under a layer of snow.

Some moss beds have taken 300 or 400 years to grow—as long as oak trees in North America.

left: A killer whale

opposite: A Weddell seal and Adelie penguins

What do people mean when they say Antarctica is a fragile environment?

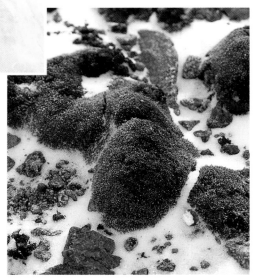

Wherever people go on the planet, they change things—by mining and hunting and fishing—and even by dropping trash. One footprint on a moss bed can last for decades, because the mosses grow so slowly.

The ways that plants and animals have survived in Antarctica have taken thousands of years to develop, and even small changes to the environment could be very harmful to them. Changes to Antarctica could then affect all the oceans and the climate of the world.

opposite: Trash left behind on old bases is now being removed.

What is being done to protect Antarctica?

Many of the world's nations have signed a **treaty** and have agreed to work together in peaceful cooperation. They are working to protect the world's greatest wilderness, now and for the future.

Ceremonial flags at the South Pole

By being aware of the world around us, being curious, and sharing our knowledge with each other, we can all make a difference. Every one of us can help to protect Antarctica.

Through our growing knowledge of Antarctica, we learn more about our world every day.

Some people say that visiting Antarctica is like visiting another world.

But Antarctica is in our world. And everyone who goes to Antarctica comes back with a great love for its beauty and a great respect for its importance.

For me, it was the greatest journey, my journey to the last great wilderness.

Glossary

antifreeze a chemical that prevents liquid from freezing, such as the antifreeze used in car engines

blubber the thick layer of fat under the skin of sea-going mammals

expedition a journey or voyage organized for a special purpose

expeditioner a person who goes on an expedition

fragile easily damaged, delicate

glaciers large masses of ice formed by compacted snow, which move slowly downhill

ice shelves the shelves of floating ice that are formed where the polar ice flows off the Antarctic continent into the ocean

moist damp, carrying moisture

plateau a high, level plain

polar having to do with the North or South Poles

treaty a legal agreement, usually between nations

wilderness a natural, unspoiled, wild area where people do not live

Index